10632232

Put Beginning Readers on the R
ALL ABOARD READ

The All Aboard Reading series is especially designed for beginning readers. Written by noted authors and illustrated in full color, these are books that children really want to read—books to excite their imagination, expand their interests, make them laugh, and support their feelings. With fiction and nonfiction stories that are high interest and curriculum-related, All Aboard Reading books offer something for every young reader. And with four different reading levels, the All Aboard Reading series lets you choose which books are most appropriate for your children and their growing abilities.

Picture Readers
Picture Readers have super-simple texts, with many nouns appearing as rebus pictures. At the end of each book are 24 flash cards—on one side is a rebus picture; on the other side is the written-out word.

Station Stop 1
Station Stop 1 books are best for children who have just begun to read. Simple words and big type make these early reading experiences more comfortable. Picture clues help children to figure out the words on the page. Lots of repetition throughout the text helps children to predict the next word or phrase—an essential step in developing word recognition.

Station Stop 2
Station Stop 2 books are written specifically for children who are reading with help. Short sentences make it easier for early readers to understand what they are reading. Simple plots and simple dialogue help children with reading comprehension.

Station Stop 3
Station Stop 3 books are perfect for children who are reading alone. With longer text and harder words, these books appeal to children who have mastered basic reading skills. More complex stories captivate children who are ready for more challenging books.

In addition to All Aboard Reading books, look for All Aboard Math Readers™ (fiction stories that teach math concepts children are learning in school) and All Aboard Science Readers™ (nonfiction books that explore the most fascinating science topics in age-appropriate language).

All Aboard for happy reading!

DISCARDED

FINCASTLE LIBRARY
11 Academy Street
P.O. Box 129
Fincastle, VA 24090

To Liam and Conor,
the founders of Snail City—Jane

To Gregg, Lynn & Micaela—R.B.

Text copyright © 2001 by Jane O'Connor. Illustrations copyright © 2001 by Rick Brown.
All rights reserved. Published by Grosset & Dunlap, a division of Penguin Young Readers Group,
345 Hudson Street, New York, NY 10014. ALL ABOARD READING and GROSSET & DUNLAP
are trademarks of Penguin Group (USA) Inc. Published simultaneously in Canada. Printed in
the U.S.A.

Library of Congress Cataloging-in-Publication Data

O'Connor, Jane.
  Snail City / by Jane O'Connor ; illustrated by Rick Brown.
    p. cm. –(All aboard reading. Level 1)
  Summary: In Snail City life is slow and the snails like it that way, all except for Gail.
  [1. Snails—Fiction. 2. Speed—Fiction.]
  I. Brown, Rick, ill. II. Title. III. Series.
  PZ7.O222 Sn 2001   2001273762
  [E] 21   CIP
                                                                      AC

ISBN 0-448-42418-5   E F G H I J

0 1191 0378403 7

ALL ABOARD READING™

Station Stop 1

Snail City

By Jane O'Connor
Illustrated by Rick Brown

Grosset & Dunlap • New York

In Snail City
life is slow.
Snails like it that way.
There is no fast food.

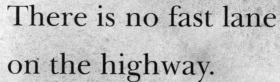

There is no fast lane
on the highway.

And it takes years
to get a letter by snail mail.

But the snails don't mind.
They like the slow life.

Well, <u>almost</u> all snails do.

This is a snail named Gail.

She is not like other snails.

Gail started to crawl before
any of the other snail babies.

Her first word was "faster."

Her mom and dad keep
on telling her to slow down.
But she can't.

Gail gets to school
early every day.

She comes in first in every race.
For snails, being first
is the worst.

16

The last one is the winner.

Today there is a class trip.
Gail is at the head
of the line.

The snail kids are going
to a flower garden.
It is five feet from school.
So it will take a long time
to get there.

Soon Gail is way ahead
of everybody.
"Fast poke!" one kid shouts.

Gail does not care.

The sun feels good.

The wind feels good.

And it feels good to crawl fast.

BOTETOURT COUNTY LIBRARY

All at once,

Gail hears something.

"Help! Help!"

Gail crawls around a rock.

Oh, no!

Far away she sees a snail baby.

The snail is going to fall

in the water!

"Hold on!"
Gail shouts.
She crawls
as fast as she can.
But it is no good.
The snail baby
has fallen in the water.
Then Gail sees a twig.
She thinks fast.
She acts fast.

Gail pushes the twig
into the water.
There is a strong wind.
Off she goes!

Gail is going fast—
very, very fast!
She has never gone
this fast before.

Gail saves the snail baby.

"Thank you!" says the snail baby.

"Thank you!"

says the snail mom.

Gail crawls back on her twig.

She goes back
across the water.
The whole snail class
is there.

"We saw what you did!"
says Ms. Slime.
"You are very brave."

No one calls her
a fast poke now.

And everyone sails on a twig.
But they wait until
there is no wind.
That way they can go…
nice and slow!